the MiLo & JAZZ
MYSTERIES®

10

THE CASE OF THE
SUPERSTAR SCAM

by Lewis B. Montgomery
illustrated by Amy Wummer

The KANE PRESS
New York

Montgomery, Lewis B.
The case of the superstar scam / by Lewis B. Montgomery ;
illustrated by Amy Wummer.
p. cm. — (Milo & Jazz mysteries ; 10)
Summary: All of Westview is excited when teen idol Starr Silveira arrives to film
an episode of her television show, but when contest winners start receiving letters
asking them to return their valuable show memorabilia, sleuths-in-training Milo
and Jazz suspect a scam.
ISBN 978-1-57565-518-5 (library reinforced binding) — ISBN 978-1-57565-519-2
(pbk.) — ISBN 978-1-57565-520-8 (e-book)
[1. Mystery and detective stories. 2. Fans (Persons)—Fiction. 3. Actors and actresses—
Fiction. 4. Swindlers and swindling—Fiction.] I. Wummer, Amy, ill. II. Title.
PZ7.M7682Cdk 2013
[Fic]—dc23
2012025268

1 3 5 7 9 10 8 6 4 2

First published in the United States of America in 2013 by Kane Press, Inc.
Printed in the United States of America
WOZ0113

Book Design: Edward Miller

The Milo & Jazz Mysteries is a registered trademark of Kane Press, Inc.

Visit us online at **www.kanepress.com**

 Like us on Facebook
facebook.com/kanepress

 Follow us on Twitter
@KanePress

Para Carolina,
una verdadera superestrella
—L.B.M.

CHAPTER ONE

Milo squeezed through the excited
crowd on Main Street. Wow! Every kid
in town seemed to be here. And half the
grownups, too.

Of course, it wasn't every day that a
TV show came to shoot an episode in
Westview. Let alone a show as popular as
Super Starr!

Everyone Milo knew tuned in each
week to watch teen idol Starr Silveira

play a singing, dancing, crime-fighting girl superhero on TV.

Usually she did it somewhere glamorous like Hollywood or Paris, France. But this time the script called for an ordinary town. And Westview was as ordinary as a town could get!

Milo spotted his friend Jazz and worked his way over to her.

"Where have you been?" Jazz asked.

"I went to the dentist after school," Milo said. "Did I miss anything?"

Jazz shook her head. "Just my brother being utterly embarrassing."

Milo followed her gaze. Jazz's older brother Chris stood by the barricade that marked off the area where the TV crew would be filming.

"Why? What's he doing?" Milo asked.

"Whenever the TV people walk by, he sticks his fist up in the air like Starr and yells, 'No time for crime!'"

"I guess he's a big fan, huh?" Milo said.

"He knows practically every episode by heart," Jazz said. "They had a trivia contest online and he won a silver guitar pick like the one Starr uses in the show."

Milo grinned. "A magic Power Pick that glows when bad guys are around?"

"I wish!" Jazz said. "That sure would come in handy on a tricky case."

Milo and Jazz were sleuths in training. They got lessons in the mail from world-famous private eye Dash Marlowe and worked together to solve mysteries that popped up in their town.

"Those Power Picks are a big deal, though," Jazz said. "Only a few hundred people won them in the whole United States. And five of them were the Woofs."

"The Woofs?" Milo repeated.

"W.F.S.S.," Jazz spelled out. "I tried calling them the Whiffs, but Chris said it sounded as if they smelled bad."

"What does it stand for?" Milo asked.

"Westview Fans of *Super Starr*. It's a fan club Chris just started at the middle school. Those new friends of his are hardcore. They've been here for *hours*."

Chris was talking now to a tall boy with uncombed hair and a wrinkled flannel shirt.

"That guy looks like he slept here," Milo said.

"Oh, Kyle always looks like that," Jazz said. "I bet his shoelaces are untied, too."

Milo glanced over, but something else caught his eye. "Are those girls wearing *flippers*?"

Two girls were posing for a boy taking their photo. One of the girls held up a magazine as they each raised a foot to show their giant rubber flippers.

"Now, Danny!" the other girl called out, teetering on one leg.

The boy with the camera gave her the thumbs-up, then clicked away.

Jazz led the way over to the girls. "Hey, Ana," she said to the one with curly hair. "How come you're wearing flippers?"

"Starr loves scuba diving!" Ana said. "Paige read it in *Teen Fad*. Right, Paige?"

"Totally." The blonde girl held out her open magazine. Milo noticed the Power Pick hanging from her leather wristband. The silver pick was decorated with a shimmering green star.

Milo and Jazz looked at the magazine. It showed Starr in a silver wetsuit with a scuba tank strapped to her back.

"We're a long way from the beach," Jazz pointed out.

"That doesn't matter," Ana said. "When Starr sees us in these flippers, she'll—she'll—"

"Flip?" Milo asked.

The boy named Danny laughed and lowered his camera. Milo saw that he wore his Power Pick on a wristband, too.

A roar went up from the crowd.

"STARR!"

"She's coming!" Ana screamed.

Danny whipped his camera back up. Everyone pressed forward. Chris leaned over the barricade and yelled, "No time for crime!"

Milo caught a flash of silver, and he strained to see around the others. Then, suddenly, he felt a hard jab in his side.

CHAPTER TWO

"Move it!" ordered the little girl who had elbowed him. Milo stumbled as she shoved past, trampling on his toes.

"Ow!" Milo grabbed his foot.

"Ursula, sweetie! Wait for Daddy!"

A bald man squeezed after her, stepping on Milo's other foot.

Yow!

Milo hopped from foot to foot.

Ignoring her father, Ursula pressed up

against the barricade. "Starr! Starr!"

Starr strode gracefully across the lot, the sun glinting off her tight silver pants. Chris and Kyle boosted Danny to their shoulders, and he snapped photo after photo from his wobbly perch.

As Starr drew near, Ana and Paige frantically waved their flippers in the air. Ana lost her balance and fell into Paige, who fell into Chris, bringing all five of the Woofs crashing to the ground.

Starr flashed a dazzling smile in their direction without breaking stride.

The Woofs picked themselves up.

"Did you all see that?" Ana gasped.

"Yeah," Milo said. "She didn't even ask if you guys were okay!"

But Ana's mind was on something

else. "She really does have silver eyes! Just like on TV!"

Paige gazed after Starr. "Totally."

Chris said, "I thought they did that with computers."

Danny looked up from his camera, which seemed to have survived the fall. "I can't believe I missed that shot!"

"Starr was moving pretty fast," Jazz said. "Doesn't she stop for autographs or anything?"

"Starr never stops to talk to fans before a shoot," Ana informed her. "Paige read it in *Teen Fad*. Right, Paige?"

"Totally."

"Why not?" Milo asked. He was beginning to wonder if Paige knew any other words.

Ana answered. "Nobody knows!"

"I bet it's an acting trick," Chris said. "To stay in character."

"What do you mean, in character?" Jazz said. "She plays herself!"

The Woofs traded glances.

"In real life she's a teen rock star," Kyle patiently explained.

Jazz said, "And on the show—"

"She plays a teen rock star *with superpowers*," Kyle said. "You see? Completely not the same!"

Jazz seemed about to say something, but a chorus of boos and hisses cut her off. *Super Starr*'s villain had arrived: The Sneer.

The Sneer prowled across the street, eyeing the crowd through his hideous, twisted mask. He let out a hollow, evil laugh. Ana and Paige shrieked.

As he passed, the little girl named Ursula turned away from the barricade. Her sharp gaze lit on Danny's wrist. She pulled her father's sleeve and pointed.

"He has a Power Pick! Like Starr!" she squealed.

"That's nice, sweetie," her father said. "Come on, we need to go."

Ursula's gaze didn't leave the pick. "*I want it.*"

"Sweetie—"

Ursula stared up at him, eyes wide. Her lower lip quivered.

"Okay, okay!" her father said hastily. He turned to Danny. "Where did you get that thing?"

"I won it in a contest," Danny said.

"Me, too." Chris held up his own leather wristband to show his silver pick. "We stayed up till midnight, to get online the minute the contest went live."

"The Power Picks come with different color stars. See?" Ana proudly displayed her sparkly magenta star. "Danny and Paige have green. Right, Paige?"

Paige nodded. "Totally."

"Kyle over there has blue." Ana pointed toward Kyle, who was hoisting himself up a stop sign for a better look at The Sneer.

"And Chris has gold," Ana went on. "At first I wanted gold, but now—"

Ursula cut in shrilly. "*I* want gold!"

Her father looked at Chris. "Okay, how much?"

"Huh?"

Ursula's father pulled out his wallet. "How much will you sell it for?"

Chris stared at him. "My Power Pick? I wouldn't sell it! Not for anything!"

"But I *want* a Power Pick, Daddy!" Ursula said.

Her father looked around the group. They shook their heads.

"Sorry," Danny said.

Ursula burst into long, loud wails. The sound reminded Milo of a siren.

As she was towed away, kicking and screaming, Ursula twisted her head and fixed the Woofs with a glare.

"I WANT A POWER PICK!" she screeched. "AND I'M GOING TO *GET* ONE!"

CHAPTER THREE

Milo quickly forgot about Ursula once the filming began. In the episode, Starr visited her ordinary cousins at their ordinary school. The TV people had changed the sign in front of Westview High School. It said "Smalltown High."

As the cameras rolled, Starr roared up on her silver motorcycle and hopped off, wearing a silver backpack. As soon as she went into the school, The Sneer oozed up and let the air out of her tires.

Milo was amazed at how many times
the actors had to repeat the scene while
the camera crew tried out different shots.
He felt sorry for The Sneer. It must be
hot inside that mask!

By 5:30 the light was fading, so filming
had to stop. The director told the actors
to be back first thing in the morning.

The next day was Saturday, so all the kids planned to return first thing as well. Milo got up early, grabbed a ripe banana, and headed out to the set.

The crowd looked even bigger today. Milo stood on tiptoe and craned his neck, hoping to spot one of his friends.

Oof!

Milo felt a hard shove. The banana flew out of his hand, and as he stumbled forward, he stepped on it. *Squish*.

Ursula marched past, clutching her father's hand and beaming up at him. Around her neck, she wore a silver chain with a Power Pick hanging from the end. The star on it was gold.

Ursula and her father disappeared into the crowd. Milo picked up his squashed

banana and headed for the nearest trash
can. As he tossed it in, Jazz came up,
looking worried.

"Have you seen Chris?" she asked.

"Not yet. Why?"

"He's been acting really strange," she
said.

"Strange how?"

"He did the dishes after breakfast."

Milo looked at Jazz. "So?"

"So, it wasn't even his turn!" she said. "And he keeps *smiling*."

"Better call 911."

"Milo, I'm serious! Something creepy is going on."

Milo wiped his hands on his jeans. "Maybe he's just psyched about *Super Starr* coming to town."

"There's something else," Jazz said. "Yesterday he got a letter. When he opened it, he looked excited. Then after dinner, he went out and wouldn't tell me where he was going." Jazz leaned forward. "And when he came back—*his Power Pick was gone*."

"That *is* weird," Milo admitted. Then

he added, "You know . . . I just saw Ursula wearing a Power Pick. And it had a gold star like Chris's."

Jazz stared at him. "Are you sure?"

Milo nodded. "You think Chris changed his mind and sold his Power Pick?"

"Chris would sell *me* if he could," Jazz said. "Cheap! But his Power Pick? No way."

It did seem unlikely. But if Chris hadn't sold his Power Pick to Ursula's father, where had it gone? And why did Ursula suddenly have one—with a gold star?

"Maybe Chris lost his Power Pick somewhere, and Ursula picked it up," Milo suggested.

"Then why is he acting so happy? And what about that mystery letter?" Jazz shook her head. "It just doesn't make sense."

Milo frowned. It was definitely puzzling. Maybe he and Jazz had found another case to solve!

During a coffee break, the crowd thinned enough for Milo and Jazz to make their way over to the Woofs. Danny was busy snapping photos of the crew and extras lining up at the food truck for muffins and Danish pastries. Milo missed his banana.

Kyle's sneakers were still untied, but Ana and Paige wore regular shoes today instead of flippers. Between them stood a spiky potted plant.

"What's that for?" Milo asked.

"Starr is a tree hugger!" Ana said.

"You shouldn't call people names for trying to save the earth," Jazz said.

"No, she actually HUGS TREES," Ana explained. "For fun. It said so in *Teen Fad*. Right, Paige?"

"Totally."

Milo eyed the potted plant doubtfully. It didn't look very huggable to him.

Just then Chris came up, and Jazz whipped around. "Did you sell that girl Ursula your Power Pick?" she demanded.

Chris gaped at her. "Are you crazy?"

"She's wearing one with a gold star," Jazz said. "And yours is gone."

All eyes went to Chris, who glanced down at his bare leather wristband.

"I didn't sell it!" he protested.

"Then where is it?" Danny asked,

letting his camera dangle on its strap.

"It's—well, it's—" Chris stopped. "Look, I'm sorry, but I just can't say."

"We *always* wear our Power Picks," Ana said. "We never take them off. Right, Paige?"

"Totally." Paige lifted her wrist to display her silver pick with its green star.

Kyle lifted his wrist too, then gave it a startled look. "Oh . . . um . . ."

Milo stared.

Kyle's wristband was bare, too.

His Power Pick was gone.

CHAPTER FOUR

"I keep forgetting that I took it off." Kyle looked around at the shocked faces. He grinned. "It's okay! She said I'd get it back."

"Who?" Jazz asked. "Ursula?"

Kyle laughed. "Of course not! *Starr.*"

Everyone stared at him.

Danny and Ana spoke at the same time.

"You talked to Starr?"

"Starr talked to *you*?"

Kyle shuffled his feet. "Well . . . no. Not exactly. But the letter—"

"Letter?" Milo asked.

"From Starr. It came two days ago. Starr said she heard I was her biggest fan in Westview. She wants me to be on the show! I get to play her sidekick in this episode."

"*What?*" Ana shrieked. "No way! How come we didn't see it in *Teen Fad*? *Teen Fad* knows ALL about *Super Starr*. Right, Paige?"

Paige looked shocked too. "T-totally," she stammered.

"It's top secret," Kyle explained. "The letter said I can't tell anybody—" He looked around at Danny, Ana, Paige, Chris, Jazz, and Milo. "Oops."

"I don't get it," Milo said. "What does this letter have to do with you not having your Power Pick?"

"Oh, Starr's going to sign it for me!" Kyle said. "I'll get it back when I go on the show."

"Chris!" Jazz said. "Are you okay?"

Chris had sunk down to the pavement. He let out a moan.

"What's wrong?" Danny asked.

Chris raised his head. Slowly, he said, "I got that letter, too. Yesterday."

Kyle looked confused. "Starr wrote to you about me being on the show?"

"No! About *me* being on the show," Chris said. "Starr promised to sign *my* Power Pick. She said *I* was her biggest fan."

"That doesn't make any sense," Danny said. "It can't be both of you. Anyway, *I'm* the biggest fan in town."

"No, *I* am!" Ana said. "Right, Paige?"

Paige scowled.

The five fans glared at each other. Even the potted plant looked spikier.

Quickly, Milo changed the subject. "Can we see the letters?"

Chris and Kyle shook their heads.

"It's not a secret anymore!" Jazz said.

"It isn't that," Chris said. "I haven't got it."

"Me neither," Kyle said. "It said to wrap my Power Pick up in the letter and leave it under the steps."

"Under the *steps*?" Milo repeated.

"Of Starr's trailer," Chris explained. "After all the TV people left for the day. Mine said that, too."

Milo and Jazz glanced at each other.

"It sounds fishy to me," Milo said.

"Me too." Jazz looked across the lot at Starr, who had finished her coffee break and stood talking to the director. "I'd like to ask her a few questions."

Quickly, Jazz ducked under the barricade and marched toward Starr. The others followed.

A young man with a tiny beard ambled over. "Can I help you?"

"We want to talk to Starr," Jazz said.

"You and everybody else. Sorry."

"You don't understand!" Chris said. "We HAVE to talk to her! She has to tell everyone I'm her biggest fan!"

"No, I am!" Kyle protested.

The young man rolled his eyes. "Fans. Honestly, I hate this job."

Ignoring their protests, he herded the group of kids back to the barricade. Danny snapped a photo as they went.

"Now what?" Kyle said when the young man had walked away.

Jazz frowned. "We have to figure out a way to get past that guy."

Thinking of Ursula, Milo suggested, "I could bump into him and make him spill his coffee. While he's distracted, you can make a dash for Starr."

"We want to talk to her," Jazz said. "Not get tackled by security."

"How about a sign?" Chris asked. "You know, like: STARR! WE NEED TO TALK TO YOU!"

Jazz gave her brother a startled look. "Actually, that's not a bad idea."

"You don't have to act so surprised," Chris grumbled.

Ana lived the closest, so they headed to her house. Ana and Paige hauled the potted plant between them.

While they were filling in the letters of their sign with black marker, Ana's mother poked her head in. "Something came for you!"

She tossed an envelope to Ana, who caught it and opened it.

"Wow," Ana said. "Wowee!"

"What is it?" Jazz asked.

Ana sat back on her heels.

"It's a letter from Starr," she said. "And it says *I* get to be on the show."

CHAPTER FIVE

Everyone clustered around Ana.

"It looks just like my letter," Kyle said.

Chris said, "Mine too."

Jazz took the envelope from Ana. "That's funny. There's no stamp."

Milo looked. "It must have been dropped off by hand."

Ana let out a shriek. "Starr was *here*? At my *house*?"

"I don't think these letters came from Starr," Jazz said.

Kyle, Chris, and Ana stared at her.

"What do you mean?" Chris said.

"It just doesn't make sense," Jazz said. "Why would she send secret letters to three fans, telling them something that can only be true for one? I think these letters are fakes."

Kyle looked bewildered. "But who would send fake letters to the Woofs? And why?"

"I don't know who," Jazz replied. "But I'm pretty sure I know why."

Milo followed her gaze to Kyle's empty wristband. Of course!

"The Power Picks!" he exclaimed. "The letters said to leave them under the steps of Starr's trailer. Whoever wrote the letters could have planned to pick them up when Starr wasn't around."

"You mean . . . it's all a scam to get our Power Picks?" Chris asked.

Ana waved her letter. "But it's signed with a little star, just like that poster on my wall. It has to be real. Right, Paige?"

Paige nodded. "Totally."

Milo looked at the poster. "Someone could have copied her signature," he said.

Ana clutched the letter to her chest. "It's not a scam. It really is from Starr. She must have changed her mind when she found out that *I'm* her biggest fan."

Chris scowled. "I hope you're right."

"You want *Ana* to get on the show?" Kyle asked.

"I want the letters to be real," Chris said. "Because if this is a scam, then *OUR POWER PICKS ARE GONE FOREVER!*"

Kyle's face fell. "Oh. Oh . . . no."

Jazz patted Kyle on the shoulder. "Don't worry," she told him. "Milo and I are on the case."

Milo took the letter from Ana's hand. "And now we have a clue!"

When they got back to the set, they saw Starr heading for the costume trailer.

"STARR!" the Woofs yelled. "STARR!" Danny and Chris held up the WE NEED TO TALK TO YOU sign while the others frantically pointed and waved their arms.

Starr turned her head. She gave them her dazzling smile, waved back—and walked on.

They all stared after her.

"So much for that," Jazz said.

"I can't understand it!" Ana said. "*Teen Fad* named Starr America's Sweetest Celebrity. They said she was 'approachable and down-to-earth.' Right, Paige?"

"Totally," Paige agreed.

"*Approachable?*" Milo repeated. "What do we have to do to get near her? Dig a tunnel? Land in a balloon?"

"Bingo!" Jazz said.

Milo looked at her in surprise, but she wasn't talking about balloons. Following her gaze, he saw Ursula perched on her father's shoulders.

"Ursula is wearing a gold Power Pick, just like you said," Jazz told him. "Let's go talk to her."

Jazz plowed off through the crowd with Milo close on her heels.

Ursula was sucking on a lollipop, her eyes glued to The Sneer, who paced the lot rehearsing lines for his next scene.

Jazz smiled up at Ursula. "That's a nice Power Pick."

The little girl glanced down at her, then away.

"Where did you get it?" Milo asked.

With a loud slurp, Ursula pulled the lollipop out of her mouth. "It's mine."

"But where did you *get* it?"

"It. Is. MINE!" Ursula slapped the lollipop down on her father's bald head.

Ursula's father gave Milo and Jazz an annoyed look. "Is there a problem?"

Milo tried not to stare at the lollipop stuck to the top of his head.

Jazz said, "We were just asking where she got her Power Pick. My brother used to have one with a gold star, too."

"Some teenage kid was selling his online," Ursula's father said.

"But Ursula didn't have one yesterday," Milo objected. "How did it get to you so fast?"

"I paid extra for overnight delivery." The man's eyes narrowed, and he crossed his arms. "What is this, anyway?"

Milo gulped. "Um . . ."

"Nothing!" Jazz grabbed Milo's arm. "We just wondered, that's all."

As she towed him away, Milo glanced back and saw Ursula pop the lollipop back in her mouth.

Once they were out of earshot, Milo asked Jazz, "Do you think he was telling the truth?"

"He *could* have bought it online," Jazz said.

"Yeah . . . or he *could* have taken Chris's Power Pick from underneath the trailer steps."

They looked at each other.

"Well . . ." Jazz said doubtfully. "I guess we could go question him again. But I didn't like the look on his face."

"Or the lollipop on his head," Milo agreed.

Jazz laughed.

"What about fingerprints?" Milo said. "There must be fingerprints all over Ana's letter."

"Yeah, but they're mostly ours—" Jazz stopped. "Ana's letter! Of course! Milo, you're a genius."

"You think the fingerprints will help?"

"No, but the letter will," Jazz said. "It will help us catch the scammer in the act."

CHAPTER SIX

"A stakeout?" Kyle asked.

The Woofs stood listening as Jazz outlined her plan.

"The three of us—" She pointed to Ana, Milo, and herself. "—come back to the set tonight after the cast and crew go home. Milo and I will hide and watch while Ana follows the instructions in the letter—"

"But the letter says to leave her Power Pick under the trailer steps!" Chris said. "What if the scammer grabs it and runs off before you guys can do anything?"

"Ana will only *pretend* to leave the letter and her Power Pick," Jazz explained. "Really it'll just be a folded-up piece of paper with a quarter taped in it."

"Then what?" Kyle asked.

"Then Milo and I wait and see who shows up after Ana leaves."

Ana frowned. "But I still think it will be Starr. If I don't leave my Power Pick, I'll lose my chance to play her sidekick on the show. I'd be a great sidekick. Right, Paige?"

Before Paige could reply, Kyle jumped in. "I got my letter first. So I'm the one who would be on the show."

"Who says?" Chris demanded.

Quickly, Milo said, "Let's think about possible suspects." He looked at Chris, Kyle, and Ana. "Who would know all three of you had Power Picks?"

Chris shrugged. "Everyone?"

"Anyone who knows us," Kyle said. "I mean, we wear them all the time."

"And Starr!" Ana said. "She knows, too."

Everybody looked at her.

"Well, she's the one who sent us the Picks when we won the contest, right?"

Jazz said, "Probably not Starr herself. But somebody at the TV show, sure."

"It could have been that guy with the strange little beard thing on his chin," Ana said. "He didn't seem too nice."

"Or The Sneer!" Kyle put in. "He's evil, right?"

Now everybody looked at him.

"The Sneer is just a TV character," Jazz said. "An actor in a mask."

"Yeah?" Kyle said. "So how come all

Starr Silveira as
Super Starr

With
**The
Sneer**

the other actors' names are listed in the credits, but for The Sneer it only says THE SNEER?"

Ana chimed in, "And no one's ever caught a glimpse of him without his mask. Not even *Teen Fad*."

"What are you saying?" Milo asked. "You think The Sneer is really evil and not just a bad guy on TV?"

"Well . . . " Ana said uncertainly.

Jazz cut in, "Whoever is sending the letters, we'll find out tonight."

"What if nobody comes?" Paige said.

Milo stared at her in surprise. Four words, and none of them was *totally*!

"They'll come," Jazz said. "The letter says to make the drop-off as soon as everyone's gone home. The scammer won't want to leave the Power Pick very long, or someone else might find it."

Ana promised to show up right after dark. Then Chris said he wanted to be in on the stakeout. Right away, the others insisted on coming too.

"It's a stakeout, not a birthday party!" Jazz said. "How are six of us supposed to hide?"

"We can be stealthy," Kyle said. "You

know that episode where Starr eludes the crazy paparazzi while she sneaks up on The Sneer? I've watched that, like, a zillion times."

Everyone started talking at once about their favorite episodes of *Super Starr*.

Jazz threw up her hands.

"Okay! You can all come. Just wear dark clothes and sneakers. And practice being quiet," she added. "Starting *now*!"

After agreeing to meet again as soon as it got dark, the group split up. By now Milo's belly was growling like an angry Doberman, so he went home for lunch.

An envelope addressed to him sat on the kitchen counter. A lesson from Dash! He tore it open and read it while wolfing down a heaping plate of leftovers.

Venn Diagrams

For a detective, gathering clues can be the easy part. Sometimes the tough part is sorting them out. Try using a **Venn diagram**. (Some people call it a "double bubble" chart!) Putting your clues in the chart helps you <u>organize what you know</u> to see how information matches up—or doesn't. For example: Milo is a boy and a detective; Jazz is a girl and a detective. A Venn diagram shows the things you have in common:

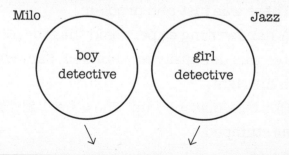

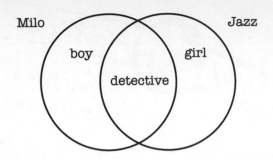

Milo   Jazz

boy   girl

detective

A double bubble helped me solve a big-league baseball case. An umpire was getting nasty anonymous letters. They were obviously from an angry baseball player—but which one?

All the clues pointed to the player known as Slammin' Sam. In a recent game, the umpire had called Sam out just as he slid into home plate. Sam had called the umpire something, too: Noodle Head. The letter writer used the same words.

There was just one problem.

A handwriting expert said that the letter writer was definitely left-handed. Sam wrote with his right.

One clue matched up. The other didn't. I was stumped.

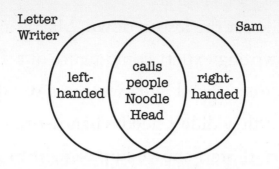

Letter Writer: left-handed

Both (overlap): calls people Noodle Head

Sam: right-handed

Sam's team had a game that afternoon. So I snapped my sleuth notebook shut and headed to the park.

As I slipped onto the bench, Sam stepped up to the plate. He tapped it with his bat and eyed the pitcher. Then he moved around to the other side of the plate.

Instantly, I was on my feet. "He did it!" I shouted, rushing from the dugout. "Sam is a switch hitter! He can use his left hand just as well as his right. That's how he wrote those letters in a different handwriting."

As the police hauled Sam away, the umpire yelled after him. He didn't call Sam names. He simply said—

"YOU'RE OUT!"

Milo set the lesson down. Maybe a
handwriting expert could figure out if
the letters signed *Starr* were real or fake?

But they didn't need a handwriting
expert. If Starr showed up tonight to get
the Power Pick, they'd know the letters
came from her. And if somebody else
showed up instead—

Then they would catch a scammer!

CHAPTER SEVEN

Milo crouched behind a trailer, thinking that six was a good number for a volleyball team, not a stakeout. So far, having the Woofs along had been nothing but trouble.

Kyle had arrived wearing silver shades just like the ones Starr wore to sneak up on The Sneer. He stumbled around in the dark and fell off the curb twice before Jazz finally made him take them off.

Then Chris and Danny, who had ducked behind the same trailer together, started squabbling.

"Darth Vader has way better powers than The Sneer!"

"Does not!"

"Does too!"

Their voices rose until Jazz had to dash across the dimly 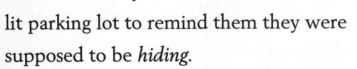 lit parking lot to remind them they were supposed to be *hiding*.

Paige crouched quietly in her spot behind the costume and makeup trailer. At least one of the Woofs wasn't causing trouble.

Milo checked his watch. Ana should

be coming along any second now to drop off her phony Power Pick and letter.

Footsteps scuffed across the parking lot. Ana was right on time.

As she came closer, they could hear her singing in a quavery voice. *"She's a superstar, oh yeah, she's Super Starr. She's got no time, no time for crime . . ."*

Milo thought she sounded nervous.

"What's she carrying?" Jazz hissed.

Milo peeked out. It was hard to make out in the dark, but it looked like . . .

"A pizza box?" he whispered.

Ana stopped in front of the trailer with the big silver stars painted on it. She leaned over and slipped something under the steps. Then she set the box on the top step.

"Look, Starr!" she announced. "Pizza! With green peas! Your favorite! Just like they make it in Brazil, where you were born. We read it in *Teen Fad*!"

Ana looked around.

"Anyway . . . I just wanted you to know that I'M YOUR BIGGEST FAN. And I BELIEVE IN YOU."

Milo shot Jazz an alarmed glance. What was Ana doing? Was she about to give away their stakeout?

"Just go now, Ana," Jazz breathed. "Go!"

As if she had heard Jazz, Ana left, singing a little louder now. "*She's got— STARR POWER! Yeah!!!*"

The minutes crawled by. Ten minutes. Twenty. Thirty-five.

Just as Milo had decided nobody was coming, he caught a movement from the corner of his eye. He grabbed Jazz by the sleeve and pointed.

A stealthy figure prowled across the parking lot.

The scammer!

All Milo could make out in the dark was that it was a man. The man paused by Starr's trailer. Milo held his breath.

But the scammer—if it was the scammer—didn't reach under the steps. Instead, after a glance at the pizza box, he turned away.

A flash exploded. Jumping out with his camera, Danny yelled, "NO TIME FOR CRIME!"

The man fled.

Milo and Jazz burst from their hiding place and sprinted after him. Milo could hear the others thundering behind.

With his long legs, Kyle soon pulled ahead. Suddenly, he went sprawling. Milo, running too hard to stop, fell over him. Then a heavy weight landed on top of Milo, pinning him down.

"Help," he gasped.

Chris's voice said, "Sorry."

The weight lifted. Milo scrambled to his feet, then helped Kyle up from the ground. Chris stood brushing himself off.

Jazz crossed her arms. "Honestly!"

"I guess I tripped on my shoelace," Kyle apologized.

The mysterious figure had vanished.

"We lost him," Milo said.

"But I got a photo!" Danny said.

They clustered around the tiny screen. The picture was blurry, and the man had his face turned away from the camera.

But Milo could tell one thing for sure. He had a full head of thick blond hair.

CHAPTER EIGHT

Jazz and Milo waited a while longer, but no one else showed up.

The next morning, Milo found Jazz finishing breakfast. Snitching a waffle, he took a big bite and said, "I still think it could have been Mister Lollipop Head. In a blond wig."

Jazz shook her head. "I realized last night—the timing doesn't work."

"What do you mean?" Milo asked.

"Well, the first day of filming was Friday. That's when Ursula saw the Power Picks and decided she wanted one, right?"

"Yeah. So?"

"Don't you see?" Jazz said. "Kyle said his letter came the day *before* that. So Ursula's father *can't* be the scammer. The letter was written before Ursula even said she wanted a Power Pick."

Hmm. She had a point.

"Then who was the mystery man?" Milo asked.

"I don't know," Jazz said. "But I'm not sure he was the scammer anyway. After all, he didn't take the Power Pick."

"He might have if Danny hadn't jumped out at him and scared him off," Milo said.

"I don't think so. He was already heading away."

"Well, if it wasn't the mystery man, then how come the real scammer never showed up to nab Ana's Power Pick? The phony Power Pick, I mean."

Jazz's eyes widened. Slowly, she said, "Maybe that's it."

"What's what?"

"Maybe the scammer *knew* that Ana wasn't really leaving her Power Pick," Jazz said. "That would be a good reason not to come."

"You mean, somebody tipped the scammer off about our stakeout?" Milo asked. "But who would do that? No one knew about it."

"No one except the Woofs," Jazz said.

Milo stared at her. "You don't think it could have been one of them!"

"They really love those Power Picks," she pointed out. "Maybe somebody wasn't satisfied with only having one. Maybe that person wanted a full set with all the different-colored stars."

Milo shook his head. "I can't believe one of the Woofs would do that. They're your brother's friends!"

"Not his regular friends," Jazz said. "He only started hanging out with them because of *Super Starr*."

Milo had to admit that it made sense. Who would want a complete set of Power Picks? A *Super Starr* fan. And a fan would know best how to trick other fans out of their Power Picks.

"The Woofs aren't the only *Super Starr* fans in Westview, though," he said. "Practically every kid in town showed up to watch the filming."

"But the scammer also has to be someone who knew about the stakeout," Jazz reminded him.

Milo buried his face in his hands. "I'm so confused."

Then he remembered Dash's lesson. Could a Venn diagram help them sort out the suspects?

He picked up Jazz's detective notebook and sparkly purple pen. Flipping the notebook open to an empty page, he drew the double bubbles.

Holy cow.

"You're right!" Milo said. "It's got to be one of the Woofs. But who?"

Jazz took the notebook and made a list of the Woofs.

Chris
Ana
Paige
Kyle
Danny

"It can't be anyone who got a letter," she said.

"Yeah," Milo agreed. "They wouldn't scam themselves out of their own picks."

Jazz crossed off the names:

~~Chris~~
~~Ana~~
Paige
~~Kyle~~
Danny

★★★★★★

She said, "That only leaves . . ."

"Danny and Paige," Milo finished. "So which one is the scammer?"

"I don't know," Jazz said. "But you and I are going to find out."

CHAPTER NINE

At Paige's house, Milo and Jazz found Paige and Ana struggling out the front door with a giant stuffed panda.

"Let me guess," Jazz said. "Starr cares about endangered species? Starr always wanted to see China?"

Ana looked puzzled. "No. She just likes big stuffed animals. Right, Paige?"

Wedged into the doorframe, Paige wheezed, "Totally." With a final heave, she and the panda both popped out.

"We need to talk to you," Jazz said to Paige.

"What's up?" Ana asked.

Jazz pulled out the double bubble chart. As she explained what it meant, Milo thought Paige looked a little sick. Ana just looked confused.

Finally Ana said, "Are you saying you think the scammer is one of *us*?"

"Not you, obviously," Jazz said. "Because you got a letter. And not Chris or Kyle."

"But that only leaves Paige and Danny!" Ana said. "And Paige would never do a thing like that! Would you?" Before Paige could respond, Ana rushed on. "It must have been Danny. He's the one who wrecked the stakeout. Right,

Paige? And he didn't get a letter, either."

"I got a letter," Paige said suddenly.

Everyone stared at her.

"You did?" Milo said.

"No way!" Ana said. "How come you didn't tell me? I can't believe you got a letter and you didn't say a—"

"Let her *talk*!" Jazz turned to Paige. "When did it come?"

"This morning, I guess. Or late last night." Paige pointed at the mail slot in the door. "When I came down, I saw the envelope lying on the floor."

She ran off to get the letter.

Ana sat down on the steps, her arm around the panda. Milo and Jazz waited. At last Paige came running back, waving a piece of paper.

Breathlessly, she said, "Here. See?"

Ana pulled her own letter from her jacket and held it next to Paige's letter. "It's exactly the same."

Milo examined the new letter. It *was* just like Ana's, down to the little star.

"I guess that settles it," Jazz said. "The scammer must be Danny."

Milo's stomach sank. He knew it made sense. The clues pointed to Danny. But Danny didn't *seem* like a scammer.

Milo could have seen Mr. Lollipop Head as the culprit. Or that grouchy young guy with the tiny beard. Or even The Sneer.

But Danny? He seemed like the kind of boy who took his friends' pictures— not their belongings.

As they walked toward the film lot, Paige and Ana carrying the panda bear, Milo kept glancing down at the letter in his hand. Something was bugging him. But what?

Turning the corner, Milo saw Danny standing with Chris and Kyle.

Dropping her side of the panda, Ana rushed toward them. Paige stumbled and fell. Milo and Jazz stopped to help her. By the time they joined the others, Ana and Danny were shouting at the top of their lungs.

"That's ridiculous!" Danny yelled. "I've already got a Power Pick of my own! Why would I try to scam you out of yours?"

Out of the corner of his eye, Milo saw crew members turning to stare at them. The young man with the little beard was pointing in their direction. He didn't look happy.

"You wanted ALL the color stars!" Ana accused. "You had green, so you got Kyle's blue, and Chris's gold, and you tried to get my magenta, and then you sent Paige—" She broke off.

Danny stabbed a finger toward Paige. "HA! Hers is green, the same as mine!

What would I want another green one
for? Huh?"

Ana looked confused, then angry. "But
you're the only one who didn't get a
letter! It HAS to be you!" She waved her
folded letter in Danny's face.

Milo looked at the letter. Then he
looked at the letter in his own hand—
Paige's letter. All at once, he knew.

"Danny didn't do it!" he announced.
"And I can prove it!"

Everyone turned to him.

"How?" Jazz asked.

Milo took Ana's letter and held it up
next to Paige's. "See? The letters aren't
the same."

Ana said, "Yes, they are! I read every
single word!"

"The words are all the same," he said. "But something else is different. Something important."

Jazz stepped forward and peered at the letters. Suddenly, her face cleared. "Oh!"

"What? I don't get it!" Kyle said.

"Paige's letter doesn't have creases," Milo explained. "It's never been folded."

Chris frowned. "So?"

"So, she said it came in an envelope, like Ana's. But it didn't. It came straight out of the printer—*her* printer."

"Paige knew we suspected her and Danny because they didn't get letters," Jazz broke in. "So she ran upstairs and printed one out—the same way she did for Kyle, Chris, and Ana."

Everyone looked at Paige, who stood silently clutching the stuffed panda.

"Paige, how could you?" Ana cried. "I thought you were my friend!"

Paige stared at the circle of faces. "You all talk so much about being fans!" she burst out. "But nobody loves *Super Starr* as much as I do."

"So you thought it was okay to steal our Power Picks?" Chris demanded.

"I had to do it!" Paige insisted. "I needed a whole set of Power Picks so I could show Starr I'm her biggest fan. That's all that matters."

"WRONG," a voice said.

They all looked up.

"Starr!" Paige exclaimed.

Starr faced them, fists on her hips, feet planted wide. She looked the same way she did on TV when she was about to flatten a bunch of bad guys.

"A real *Super Starr* fan would never steal," she said. "Because a real fan always remembers the *Super Starr* motto—"

She paused, and everyone chimed in.

"NO TIME FOR CRIME!"

CHAPTER TEN

Milo yawned and rubbed his eyes as he hurried down Main Street. The letter said to meet outside Starr's trailer at six a.m. sharp. It wasn't signed, but he was sure it came from Jazz.

She was already waiting there.

"All right," he said. "What's up?"

Jazz looked confused. "What do you mean? You left a letter telling me to meet you here."

"Huh? I thought *you* wrote—"

He broke off as Kyle, Chris, Ana, and Danny came up.

"What are you doing here?" Milo asked.

Jazz said, "Did you get letters too?"

The Woofs exchanged glances.

"We thought they came from you," Chris said.

Danny looked around and groaned. "Oh, no. Not Paige again."

"She already gave back our Power Picks," Kyle said. "And she told us she was sorry."

"Besides, she's grounded," Ana said. "Her parents won't even let her come out to watch the filming." She shook her head sadly. "Who would have guessed a *Super Starr* fan could go so wrong?"

A car pulled up. A blond man got out and started toward a trailer.

Milo stared. Hey! Wasn't that—

"The mystery man!" he exclaimed.

The man turned. Seeing the camera hanging from Danny's neck, he threw his arms over his face. "No pictures! Please!"

"Huh?" Danny said. "Why would I want to take your picture?"

"Who *are* you?" Jazz asked the man.

"I guess they don't know you without the mask!" a new voice said.

They all turned.

A smiling teenage girl stood on the steps of Starr's trailer. It was Starr. But there was something different about her.

"Your eyes!" Ana exclaimed. "They're brown!"

Starr laughed. "Sure. The silver contact
lenses are part of my costume." She made
a face. "Not my favorite part, either. The
way they slip around, half the time I
can't see a thing!"

Now Milo understood why she hadn't seen their sign asking to talk with her. That must be why she never stopped for autographs, either.

Starr gestured toward the blond man. "This is Jim. He plays The Sneer."

Everyone stared at him.

"I know," the man said gloomily. "Sometimes I hardly believe it myself."

Starr came down from the steps and flung her arm around his shoulders. "Poor old Jim. He'd rather be in some wacky experimental play than on TV."

"You kids just don't appreciate art," Jim said.

"Art!" Starr appealed to the others. "The last play he was in, he sat with his back to the audience and didn't say a

word! For three hours straight!"

"At first, it was five hours," Jim said. "But we trimmed the script."

"Did lots of *Super Starr* fans come to see your play?" Jazz asked.

Jim looked horrified. "Certainly not!"

"He keeps his role on *Super Starr* a secret," Starr explained. "He's afraid if people in the off-off-off-off-Broadway world knew that he played The Sneer, they wouldn't take him seriously anymore."

"But The Sneer rocks!" Kyle said. "Ask any kid in town."

Jim winced. "My point exactly. Serious actors do not *rock*."

So that was why they had seen him sneaking around the lot, Milo realized. And why Jim had run when Danny snapped his picture.

"But who sent the letters telling us to meet here?" Milo asked.

"I did, of course!" Starr said.

"What for?" Jazz asked.

Starr disappeared into her trailer. She returned carrying a pair of silver jackets. Each had *Starr Power* embroidered on the back. She handed one to Jazz and the other to Milo.

"Wow, thanks!" Jazz said.

"You deserve them!" Starr told them. "I fight crime on TV. But you two fight crime in real life!"

Milo put on his jacket. Awesome! He wondered if Dash Marlowe had ever gotten a present from a TV star.

"How come you wanted us here too?" Chris asked.

Starr smiled. "I felt bad that you'd all gotten those scam letters saying you could be on *Super Starr*. So I talked to my director, and she had the writers tweak the storyline for this episode. You're going to be my band!"

"All four of us?" Danny asked.

Starr nodded, and they cheered.

"But I don't play an instrument!" Kyle said.

"That's okay," Starr said. "My guitar pick isn't really magic, either. It's TV. You can just pretend."

An hour later, Milo and Jazz sat in directors' chairs sipping steaming cocoa that the young man with the tiny beard had brought them from the food truck.

They were watching Starr lip-synch a song while her new band enthusiastically "played" for the camera. Chris tossed his drumsticks in the air and caught them. Ana did a duck walk with her bass.

Jazz leaned over to Milo. "So—the Case of the Superstar Scam is closed," she said. "And I think this is our best ending for a case yet. Don't you?"

Milo grinned.

"Totally!"

SUPER SLEUTHING STRATEGIES

A few days after Milo and Jazz wrote to Dash Marlowe, a letter arrived in the mail. . . .

Greetings, Milo and Jazz,
    Congratulations on solving—yes!—your *tenth* case! I'm proud of you two. You've retrieved a lucky talisman (remember those stinky socks?), exposed a phony psychic, nabbed a thief, saved an election, unmasked a scammer. . . . I can't help wondering what will be next!
    Of course, you don't want to slack off now. Stay in shape with these tricky puzzles and mini-mysteries!

Happy Sleuthing!
—*Dash Marlowe*

Warm Up!
Rev up your minds with these brain stretchers. (I won't insult you by telling you where to find the answers. . . .)

1. How many numbers between one and one hundred have an *a* in their spelling?
2. How can a man go 10 days without sleep?
3. What two keys can't open any lock? (Hint: Think animals.)
4. What happened in 1961 that won't happen again until the year 6009?

Spot the Difference: An Observation Puzzle

This is the evil Dinoman, movie monster extraordinaire. The actor who plays him has a double who does some of his tough stunts. Naturally, the Dinoman costume and the stunt double's costume should look exactly alike. But oops! The costume department got careless. See if you can spot the six differences!

Dinoman   **Dinoman double**

Answer: Dinoman has curved horns, curved teeth, a ring on one claw, no heel on his right boot, no design on his shirt, and no spikes on his tail. The Dinoman double has straight horns, pointed teeth, no ring, heels on both boots, a design on his shirt, and three spikes on his tail.

Scammed: A Logic Puzzle

 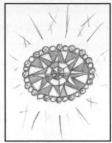 

Three ex-robbers knew a lot about crime, but they still got scammed! See if you can figure out what each guy was fooled into buying and what he did with what he bought.

Look at the clues and fill in the answer box where you can. Then read the clues again to find the answer.

Answer Box (*see answers on next page*)

	Rocky	Louie	Sal
What he bought			
What he did			

1. One guy was scammed into thinking he'd bought the Brooklyn Bridge. When he found out, he tried to trade it for the Golden Gate.
2. Louie was not the one who bought a big diamond that was actually made of glass.
3. Sal paid a bundle for "beautiful waterside property!" (It turned out to be underwater.)
4. Rocky just kept what he bought, because it was so pretty.
5. One guy borrowed a boat.

Something Fishy: A Mini-Mystery

Every criminal lies. So naturally, every detective has to be ready to spot a lie. Read this, turn on your mental lie detector, and draw a conclusion!

I was strolling around the city aquarium when I ran into a client, Myra Hode, who was about to inherit a lot of money. She was

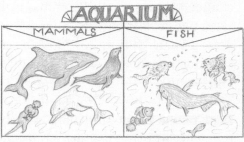

with a tall, thin, bearded man. With great excitement she said that he was her long-lost cousin, Ezra, who had suddenly appeared—just in time to share her inheritance! Ezra was a scientist who had disappeared 10 years earlier when he tried to cross the Pacific alone in a small sailboat. The man smiled and told me a dramatic story of being marooned on a tiny island, barely surviving until he was finally rescued. "For a scientist it had its upside," he said. "Observing wildlife close up. Beautiful seabirds. Huge fish, like whales and dolphins. Sharks, of course . . ."

I turned to Myra and said, "This man is a fake. Don't give him one dime." How did I know?

Answer: Any scientist would know that whales are mammals, not fish. "Ezra" turned out to be the notorious con man Freddie the Faker.

Answer to Logic Puzzle: When Louie realized he'd been scammed, he tried to trade the Brooklyn Bridge for the Golden Gate. Rocky bought the fake diamond and held onto it because it was so pretty. Sal snapped up the waterfront property. When he found out it was underwater, he simply borrowed a boat!

107

Dash's Dilemma: A Venn Diagram Puzzle

It was vacation time and I knew what I wanted—a faraway place with great beaches and plenty of criminals to catch (in case I got bored). That was a challenge. But I used a Venn diagram, and in no time I had two perfect choices. Take a look at these lists, draw a Venn diagram (or "double bubble" chart), and see what my choices were. Then I'll tell you where I ended up!

High Crime Rate! Mugville, Crooksville-by-the-Sea, Smuggler's Cove, Thugtown, Burglar's Beach, Mayhem, Cape Felony, Robber's Lagoon

Great Beaches! Silver Sands, Nemo Bay, Mermaid's Delight, Burglar's Beach, Sandy Landing, Smuggler's Cove, Luna's Lagoon, Catfish Coast

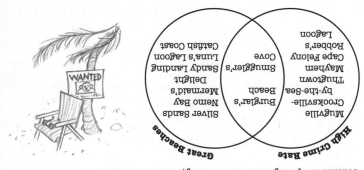

Great Beaches

Silver Sands
Nemo Bay
Mermaid's Delight
Sandy Landing
Luna's Lagoon
Catfish Coast

Burglar's Beach
Smuggler's Cove

High Crime Rate

Mugville
Crooksville-by-the-Sea
Thugtown
Mayhem
Cape Felony
Robber's Lagoon

Answer: Burglar's Beach and Smuggler's Cove. Each has gorgeous beaches and plenty of crime. Obviously, I had to visit both.

Answers to Brain Stretchers:
1. None. (Try it yourself!)
2. He sleeps at night.
3. A donkey and a monkey.
4. You can read the year upside down!

Don't miss book #11 in
The Milo & Jazz Mysteries:

The Case of the Locked Box

Someone stole 100 dollars from a locked cashbox . . .
and almost everyone in school thinks the culprit is
Jazz! When Jazz is put on trial in student court, it's up
to Milo to prove her *not guilty*. And that's no easy task,
since Jazz is the only person at school with a key!
But if Jazz is innocent, as Milo knows she is, then how
could someone else have gotten into the locked box?
And who? The mystery—and the trial—are on!

COMING SOON
More mysteries from your favorite kid detectives!

Visit **www.kanepress.com/miloandjazz.html**
to see all titles!

a great addition to elementary school and public libraries."
—*Library Media Connection*

#5: The Case of the July 4th Jinx
2011 Moonbeam Children's Book Award Silver Medalist
"Excellent summer reading." —*Midwest Book Review*
"A good choice." —*School Library Journal*

#6: The Case of the Missing Moose
"Engaging . . . Fun pen-and-ink illustrations enhance
the story. Numerous clues are provided, a red herring
is present, and the mystery has a surprising twist at
the end." —*Booklist*

#7: The Case of the Purple Pool
"Young readers might just have to exercise their brains to
solve this one. I think mystery fans ages 6–10 will enjoy
this series." —*Semicolon blog*

#8: The Case of the Diamonds in the Desk
"Sprightly illustrations enliven the brief chapters, which
are filled with earnest, clever kids being funny—and,
more importantly, smart. . . . Ends with a series of highly
enjoyable brain teasers." —*Booklist*

#9: The Case of the Crooked Campaign
"A hilarious circus of clues . . . Humorous
illustrations add to the fun and kids will
have a fantastic time keeping up with the
sleuthing action of Milo and Jazz."
—*Midwest Book Review*

Collect these mysteries
and more—coming soon!

**Visit www.kanepress.com
to see all titles in
The Milo & Jazz
Mysteries.**

ABOUT THE AUTHOR

Lewis B. Montgomery is the pen name of a writer whose favorite authors include CSL, EBW, and LMM. Those initials are a clue—but there's another clue, too. Can you figure out their names?

Besides writing the Milo & Jazz mysteries, LBM enjoys eating spicy Thai noodles and blueberry ice cream, riding a bike, and reading. Not all at the same time, of course. At least, not anymore. But that's another story. . . .

ABOUT THE ILLUSTRATOR

Amy Wummer has illustrated more than 50 children's books. She uses pencils, watercolors, and ink—but not the invisible kind.

Amy and her husband, who is also an artist, live in Pennsylvania . . . in a mysterious old house which has a secret hidden room in the basement!